CONTENT :

The perplexing door

Drill... drill... I think you can hear that piercing sound of the drilling machine. There is some work going on in my house. Swaraaa..., wait, my mom is calling, I will come back... (a few moments later). So, where was I? Yes, there is some carpentry work going on in my house and my mom has sent me to the basement to get a carpenter's kit. Ouch, I tripped over something but what's that, a secret door. I will figure it out later. I got the kit and went to my mom, I did not find it necessary to tell mom about the secret door but if the matter goes serious then I will definitely tell it to my parents.

After that, I went into the basement and started to find the secret door. Four minutes later I found the secret door. When I was about to open the door, my mom called me and asked me where were you, I answered, "I was in my bedroom."My mother said "I was in the bedroom just a while ago." I said "I was in the backyard."My mother said "I did not see you going there." I said "I was in the living room." And I went into my study room after saying this and started to study. It was already evening and my dad came home. My mom called me at 8 p.m. for supper and I thought to explore the perplexing door tomorrow because I think exploring a whole lot of secrets and mysterious things in the morning is a better option. At the dinner table, I saw my mom looking at me with a skeptical look. When I had my supper I went to bed and started to read a book. When I felt somnolent, I felt myself falling into slumber.

I woke up in the morning and yawned like anything. I got ready and went to school. When I reached school, I met my mathematics teacher and was happy. After the class teacher's time, it was a biography class and we needed to go for a nature walk. We all got ready with our books and pens, our teacher came and took us all to the nature walk. Now it was French class, our teacher was absent, so we got a free class. We played ice and water in our class and stole each other's water bottles. After some classes, it was lunch time, my best friend met me and I told her about the secret door. She gave me an idea to figure out the secret door together when my parents would be busy and they would be out of the house. The lunch time was over and I was thinking about the secret door all the time and was not paying attention to the classes. My teachers were not happy to see me behave like this, that is why they complained to my mom about this behaviour. I reached home after the school ended and when I was going in the basement, my dad told me to get ready because we needed to go to my cousin's house for supper.

BACK TO
SCHOOL

Statues and Cats

So I got ready and wore a purple dress which had a flower design. We went to my cousin's house and we played many games and had our supper. The next day, I went to the school and went to my class. I was thinking that I should call my friend and we both could figure out the mystery, thinking that I bumped into a wall and my classmates mocked me. At lunch time I told my friend why I could not explore the secret door.

After lunch time, I attended my classes and went home. When I reached home, I saw my mom and dad getting ready and I asked them where they were going. They told me that they had some work in the neighbouring city which was about ten kilometers away from my city. Then my mind started working and after my parents left, I called my friend and asked her to come to my house. When my friend came, my friend and I got ready with tools. We got helmets, a drilling machine if needed, a torch because we were not sure that we would use it but we kept it for safety, a rope and a digital watch because my parents were coming home at 4:00. We also took water bottles and some snacks. By the time we found the secret door it was already 2:30. We hurried and went inside the secret door. Ouch, I bumped into my friend. It was so dark there that my friend and I were not able to see each other. We both took out the torches and looked at each other. We looked each and everywhere, side by side, up and down.

We were very scared because there were statues everywhere around us. There was no way to get out of the room except the secret door. We decided to explore the secret door, sorry the secret room more. We examined each and every statue meticulously and were shocked at the skills of the artist who had made the statues because they were so real that anybody seeing them at the first site could say that this is a human but has fallen in mud. On the spur of the moment, we heard cats meowing. We both started looking here and there. We were reasoning that from where the cats had come. Just then the alarm of my digital watch started ringing. I had set the alarm for 3:50 p.m. on my watch. We hurried and took out the rope and climbed it. Just as we reached the living room, the doorbell rang. We opened the door and found out that it was the postman uncle ringing the bell. After sometime my parents came, me and my friend greeted them, I told them that I had called my friend because I wanted to play with her and we both started to play.

3. Vanishing

It was almost 5:30 p.m. and my friend had already left my house. I started studying because I did not have some work to do. I studied for one hour and then I practiced dancing. Now it was supper, my parents were talking about the mall which had opened just three weeks ago and were planning to go there tomorrow. I went to bed after having supper. I was excited and sad because I wanted to go to the mall but I needed to explore the secret room. I woke up in the morning and I went to eat my breakfast, my parents told me that I was also going with them. I acted like I was having a stomach ache, my mom said "no problem I stay at home if you say" I said "you both go to the mall, I will stay at home". My parents went to the mall after some time, I called my friend and told her everything. She came to my house rapidly, just as she entered my house, the doorbell rang, we opened it and saw the carpenter uncle .

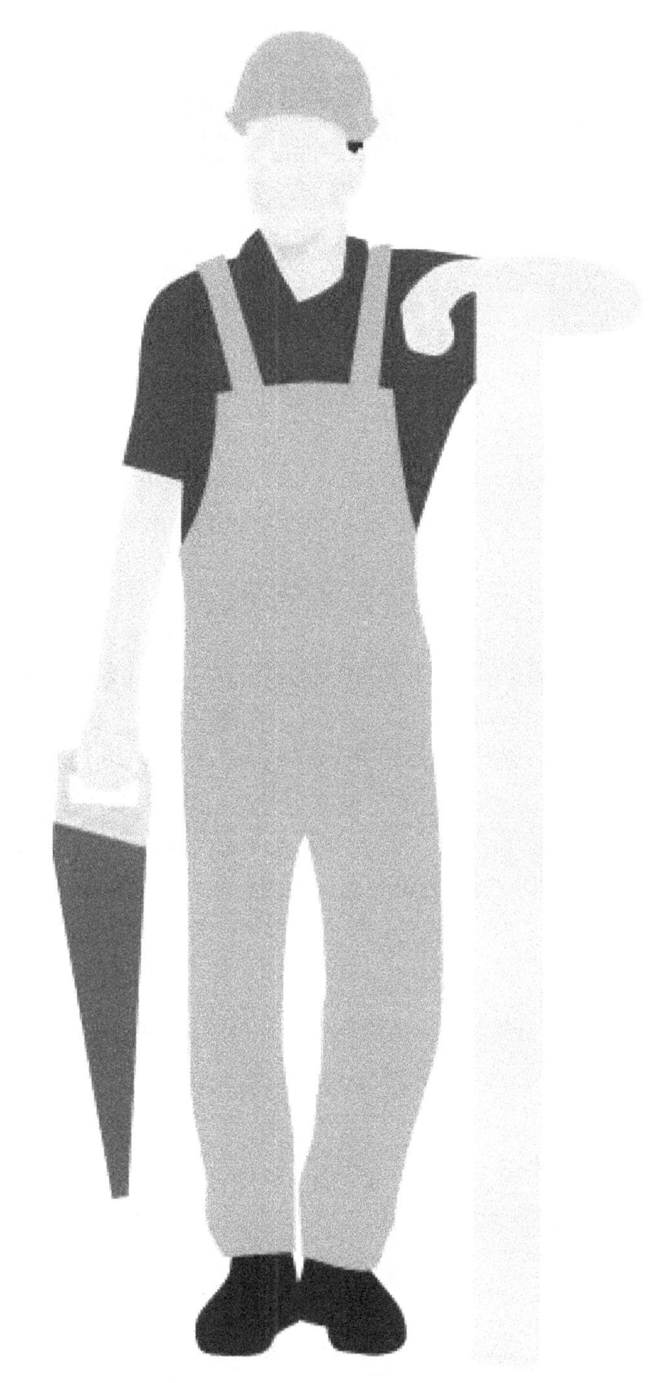

The carpenter uncle said "Is sir and madam home?"
I said "no" he said "They told me to come to work
today. " I was wondering what I should tell him so
that he does not work today. Then I had an idea and
I told him that my parents had told me to tell you
that today you cannot work because I am sick and if
there is some dust in the house, I will get more sick.
Later he went and we got ready. This time we were
taking a torch, helmets, and hammer because we
needed to check the statues, a digital watch, water
bottles, a rope and a dog. If the cats attack us we will
be having a dog to avert. We were able to search the
secret door easily because we marked the place
where the secret door was. We went through the
secret door with our torches on. We landed on the
ground safely because we were able to see the land
clearly. We both looked around but we were not able
to see any of the statues, we even thought that they
were invisible but they vanished. We got to know
this because we ran in the whole room but the room
was empty.

It was a good thing that all the statues were not there because now we were able to see a narrow passage. It was also shocking how anybody could take all the statues in one day because we left the secret door at 4:00 the day before and we returned today at 10:30. Forget that, we both accompanied by the dog started to walk on the narrow passage as we walked some steps and our dog disappeared. We both were appalled to see the dog vanish in thin air. We both ran and climbed the rope and now we were in the basement. We were reasoning that we should tell it to my parents. My friend was very sad because the dog was her's and what will she tell her parents.

4. Advent

As we went out of the basement, we felt very hungry. As we started walking towards the kitchen, the statues that were in the secret room appeared here and the statues were everywhere in the house. From the living room to the kitchen and from the bedroom to the basement, but the shocking thing was that they were not in the secret room and its surrounding areas. We were wondering why the dog didn't appear. Instantaneously, a barking sound was heard by us and we began searching in each and every corner of the house. Soon, we found the dog buried inside the statues and we took him out. Later, we thought about the statues and tested them but how could we move every statue from there. Subsequently, my friend and I tried to lift one statue together. That statue was so light in weight that one of us was enough to lift it and we were appalled to see this magic. So, we started working, one by one we lifted the statues but the statues were copious.

We were able to shift only the statues of the living room to the secret room. In that instant, the bell rang and we were ready to tell our parents about the secret door and secret room. We opened the door with a very sad look on our face. As we opened the door, we saw the carpenter uncle and asked him "why are you here?" he said "I asked sir about the work and he said that I should go to work." My friend had an idea and she said "uncle, can you help us shift these statues." The uncle asked "but from where did you bring these statues, can I take them because I can sell them in the market."We said "of course!!!" Then, we all started shifting the statues from our house to the truck because we were three people now, so it was as easy as falling off a log to shift the statues. We were relaxed and happy about this thing and we thought about continuing tomorrow after school.

While the uncle left. We both were watching television and the bell rang. We opened the door and my parents entered, we greeted them and after sometime my friend went. My parents scolded me about telling the carpenter uncle to not work today. I had my supper and went to bed.

5.The secret is not a secret anymore

I woke up in the morning and got ready for school. My best friend was not there at school and I was very bothered.When I arrived at my home, my mom opened the door and I asked her why she was at home. I enquired about my friend and was relieved to hear that she was blooming. I asked her mom to send her to my home.

When my friend arrived at my home, we started making a plan to send my mom out of the house. Soon, we got an idea and the idea was to call my mom with my father's old sim card. So we started to make some arrangements and called my mom and asked her to go to the dad's office. When my mom left we went into the basement with a torch and a rope. As we went inside the secret door, we saw that narrow passage that we had seen. And started walking on that passage. We walked for miles and saw a mall which looked jinxed. We went inside the mall and saw a chandelier moving to and fro. We ignored that and started to continue our journey. As we went upstairs we saw a frame having a photo of a stranger girl. As we were looking at the photo, a crying sound was heard by us. We started to follow the sound and we reached the room from where the sound was coming. We peeped through the room and saw a translucent girl who was crying.

We were shaking like a leaf and ran downstairs. We ran till halfway of the passage and were exhausted. We walked to the secret room and climbed the rope. We thought of telling this to my parents. And as we came out of the basement, the bell rang. We opened the door to find my mom and told each and everything to her. In the evening my dad came home and my mom told him the whole story. They got angry with me for not telling them about this incident. I had my supper and went to bed. I was able to hear my parents talking very seriously about this matter and they slept. I was thinking about what would happen tomorrow.

6.Following the ancient magic

The next day I woke up and as usual, got ready. When I went downstairs, my mom told me to change my dress because I was not going to school. This was the first time my mom told me to stay at home without a reason. I went into my room and changed my clothes. I went downstairs again and just as I was sitting on the chair, my mom told me to bring my books. As I came to the dining table after giving my mom the books, my dad told me to bring his glasses. I was worn out. I had my breakfast and I watched the news with my parents. I asked my mom "why you advised me to stay at home", my mom answered "we need to discuss something with you."My dad stared my mom with a confused look. My dad started to changed the topic and talked about the recent World Cup, which India won. I was dancing when India won the World Cup.

Just then my mom told me to get a shower. I went into the lavatory and got a shower. It was around 12:30 when I came downstairs. I had my lunch and my mom advised me to take a short nap because I was bored. I took a long nap instead of a short nap and I woke up at 5:00. Then I asked my mom "why didn't she send me to school?" My mom replied "we wanted you to rest at home." I already knew that my mom would tell me a lie.

I was helping my mom in cutting the veggies for dinner. And my mom told me that we will follow the ancient magic that my grandmother suggested. I asked her, "Which thing will we use for the magic? My mom replied "it depends on the secret door or that house."Now it was night and I went to bed after having my supper. The next day I woke up and went to school. I sat in the bus and was thinking about the ancient magic and secret door. I did not find it necessary to seal the secret door because it was not causing any harm and nobody was troubled with it. I attended school and went home by bus. As I reached home, I saw my mom and carpenter uncle at home. I went to my room to freshen up a bit. As I was about to change, there was a sound of somebody falling. Me and my mom went into the basement because the sound was coming from there. I already knew that the carpenter uncle would fall through the secret door. I went inside the secret door and my mom in the basement above the secret door.

7. An accident

As I went in the secret door, I began to search for the carpenter uncle. I found him on the passage and held his hand. I pushed him till the opening and tied him from the rope. I gave my mom a signal to pull the rope up and I also started pushing him. We were successful in taking him out. After the carpenter uncle was taken out, my mom took me out of the secret door. We went into the living room and gave a glass of water to the uncle. We were flabbergasted to see the carpenter uncle behave like a cat. We got to understand this because he was not drinking the water normally like a human, he was licking the water like a cat and he was also saying "meow, meow." We took him to the hospital and called his family. His family was crying because the doctor told us that he was very frightened to see something which was scary, so he got paralyzed and his mind stopped working.

We went home after the incident and told everything to my father when he came home. Now I was thinking that it is very important to seal the secret door. During supper, my parents and I discussed the incident and decided that tomorrow my father will come home early from the office and we all will explore the secret door. I went to bed after having my supper. The next morning I woke up and as usual went to school. I attended the school and reached home after the school ended.

My parents were there at home and I went to my room to freshen up. I was also wondering why me and my friend did not get paralyzed or something else. But it was a good thing that we were safe. After some time me and my parents went to the secret door and went inside. I told my parents about the room where the statues were kept. We all walked through the passage and reached the haunted place. We went inside it and tried to find the lights. It was dark all around and we were able to see each other by the torches. We saw the to and fro moving chandelier and I told my parents about it. We went upstairs and saw a picture of an unknown girl. My mom told us that the girl was appearing similar to her and she had seen her. We started exploring the rooms and we saw a room with a big button and two huge statues. I tried to press it and the whole house started to jiggle.

We all balanced and after a while, the house changed to a theatre. We went outside the haunted theatre to see if it changed from outside. It was the same as before and we all went to the opening after checking this. We climbed up the rope and went into the living room. When we reached the living room, we all relaxed. Now it was already supper, we all had supper and went to bed.

8.Time for magic

The next morning, I woke up and got ready for school. Just as I went downstairs, I saw an uncle who was wearing an orange coloured t-shirt which had a ghost design and a blue coloured trouser. As I was going out of the house to catch the bus, the uncle stopped me from going out. My mom explained to me that the uncle was a priest who was an expert in getting rid of ghosts and that he can seal any door. I asked why he is not letting me go out of the house. My mom replied I do not know, he said this to us too. I changed my clothes and my mom reported to my teacher that I will not come to school. I was having doubts about the priest because he was looking very cunning and clever. I observed him carefully and analyzed each move. I also took a cautious look at every object that the priest had touched. I had my breakfast and during that breakfast, my mom told me that my grandmother had sent him to our house.

So I was wondering why my grandmother believed in a person who looked cunning and clever. I was really not comfortable having the priest at our home because every action of him seemed to look complex. After having my breakfast, I relaxed and watched television. After some time, my mom told me to switch off the television and start doing my homework. I went into the study room and opened my mathematics book. The homework in mathematics was a worksheet based on fractions. After completing it, I opened my english notebook to write a comprehension as mentioned in the homework. I completed the comprehension and then I was free. I was about to have my lunch, but my mom called me and told me to call my dad on his phone and tell him to come home. I asked her why she was in a hurry. My mom replied the priest is saying that every member of the house should be present.

I called my dad and I told him to come home urgently. My dad came home in fifteen minutes. We all sat near the priest and he said that he wanted to explore the secret door. So, me and my parents, along with the priest went into the secret door and we told him each and everything that had happened. I told him about the room and the statues. We started walking on the passage and the priest observed everything rigorously. In some time we all reached the haunted house which had turned into a haunted theatre. We went inside the house but the house was no more a theatre and the same thing repeated. The chandelier moved to and fro. We all went upstairs and looked at the picture of the girl. The priest asked if by chance we knew that girl or met her in the past. My mom said that she had seen that girl before and knew her but she cannot remember her. We all observed all the rooms prudently. We went outside the house and reached the opening. We went through the secret door and now we were present in the basement.

The priest was now ready with all the things. He said that he would ask some questions and we need to answer the questions honestly during the magic. So, we all sat near the four corners of the secret door. The priest muttered some words which we were not able to hear. He signaled us that the ancient magic had been started. He started saying that we need to seal the secret door and peeped inside the secret door. A sharp voice came out and said why you want to seal the secret door. The priest started to ask questions to us but we were allowed to answer in a single word. He asked who saw the secret door first? I answered "me", his next question was "were you with someone? " I said "yes", he asked "who was that person?" I said "friend". The priest now said "you answer in detail now", he asked "why you did not tell this to your parents?" I answered, "I did not find it necessary to tell it to my parents because nothing scary was happening."

This was the last question of the priest and he sealed the door with a strong lock and the key was invisible but it was visible to us only.

9. What ?

Now the secret door was sealed and the priest went after drinking tea. My parents were now relieved and happy. My mom was very tired so my dad ordered food from Zomato. We ordered spring rolls, Momos, Manchurian, a brownie and two pastries. The food came and we ate it. After having my supper I went to bed. The following morning, I woke up and as usual got ready for school but I forgot that today was Sunday. So, I went downstairs and had my breakfast. I watched television and read the newspaper. I went to my room to get a nice bath. After taking a bath, I went downstairs and ate my lunch. My mom was cleaning the house and she went in the basement to clean it and she saw the secret door locked properly. After the cleaning, my mom sent me to the basement to get some tools for gardening. I saw the tools and picked them. In a flash, my sharp eyes went on the secret door which was opened.

I gave my mom the tools and told her about the secret door. She went into the basement to see the secret door and when she saw it, she was tense. Suddenly, I saw a shadow passing. I told this to my mom. She called my dad at once. My mom started preparing supper. My dad came and we all had our supper. We went to bed after having our supper. The next morning, I woke up and went to school. I attended the school and reached home. The priest was at our home and he was examining every room of our house. Abruptly, he saw a dark shadow moving past him but the shadow disappeared in a few seconds. The priest went to the neighbouring room and saw the shadow there, he started to follow the shadow. The shadow was looking like a girl's figure but only the shadow was visible, not a girl. When me and the priest were following the shadow, my mom was working in the kitchen. We followed the shadow but after some time, we got to know that the shadow was looking for my mom and it went in the kitchen.

When we had reached the kitchen, we saw my mom scared and the shadow was not moving.

The priest had an idea and he whispered something in my and my mom's ears. He whispered that he would do some magic to catch the shadow and then we could talk to the shadow. The priest also told us to stay there because if it started moving, we could follow it and he predicted that the shadow would not move because it was following my mom. After some time, the priest came with a glass bottle and a lighted candle. He started to utter some words and then he asked the shadow if it would come inside the glass bottle. The shadow went inside the bottle without reacting like a good spirit. After some time, my dad came and we told everything and showed him the glass bottle containing the spirit. The priest said that we would talk to the spirit on the following day, when everybody would be present at home. He also said that we could not talk to the spirit in the night because the spirits are stronger at night. The priest went after saying this and we had our supper. After having our supper we went to bed.

The following morning, I woke up with a shock because I had seen a nightmare. I got ready for school and went to school. I attended all classes and reached home after school ended. When I reached home, I saw the priest, my dad and my mom at home. I got freshen up and came downstairs to eat some snacks. After eating snacks, me, the priest, my dad and my mom went into the basement. We went through the secret door. We started walking on the passage and we arrived at the door of the haunted house. We went inside the house and we went upstairs. We looked at the photo but the girl in the photo had disappeared. We were appalled to see this. We went outside the house and started walking on the passage. We reached the opening and then we went through the secret door. Now we were in the basement and we went into the living room. The priest told us that the shadow is of that girl which was in the photo. So, after our comfort, we sat near a lighted candle and there was the glass bottle containing the spirit.

When the magic had started, we took out the bottle cap and the black shadow came out in a bigger form. The priest uttered some words and now the shadow seemed to understand our motive. The priest asked the shadow "who's shadow are you?" The shadow replied in a sharp voice "the girl you saw in the photo." The priest asked, "so you are the spirit of that girl." The shadow replied "yes." After saying this the shadow changed into a transparent girl which my friend and I had seen. The shadow started saying to me "I was once alive and I was the elder sister of your mom. I died on the day when your mom was borned. From that moment, I became a spirit and searched for my sister, that's why I came to your house and made a secret door which you discovered. Now my wish has been fulfilled, so I can go back." She went near my mom and hugged her for the last time. After she left, my mom got a call from the carpenter uncle and he said that now he was well and he can come back to work. Everything was now okay and I was also happy that my mom had heard the truth after these many years.